I DID IT!

Pirates Can Be Honest

Written by
Tom Easton

Illustrated by
Mike Gordon

WAYLAND

Some days you're better off just staying in bed. But staying in bed wasn't an option for poor old Davy Jones the day his hammock snapped! His day soon got worse.

I DID IT!

Pirates Can Be Honest

First published in 2014 by Wayland

Text © Wayland 2014
Illustrations© Mike Gordon

Wayland
338 Euston Road
London NW1 3BH

Wayland Australia
Level 17/207 Kent Street
Sydney, NSW 2000

Commissioning editor: Victoria Brooker
Creative design: Basement68

A catalogue record for this book is
available from the British Library.
Dewey number: 823.9'2-dc23

ISBN 978 0 7502 8295 6
Ebook ISBN 978 0 7502 8556 8

Printed in China

10 9 8 7 6 5 4 3 2 1

Wayland is a division of
Hachette Children's Books,
an Hachette UK company.
www.hachette.co.uk

Captain Cod asked Davy to clean the
cannonballs below deck.
"But Captain," Davy said. "Cleaning
cannonballs is the worst job on the ship."

"Sorry Davy," the Captain said, "but if there's
one thing I insist on, it's clean cannonballs.
Be careful that you don't drop any!"

Davy went down into the hold and sighed
as he saw the huge pile of cannonballs.
"They're heavy and greasy and there are just
so many of them," he said to himself.
"This is going to take forever!"

But there was nothing else for it.
Davy got to work. He scrubbed, spat
and shined. As the cannonballs
got cleaner, he got dirtier.

As the day went on, Davy grew hungry and tired.
He began day-dreaming about having
a nice bubble bath before dinner. In fact,
Davy was so busy day-dreaming, he dropped a
particularly heavy cannonball on his big toe.

Davy hopped around clutching
his foot and saying some rude words.
Meanwhile, the cannonball rolled right
through an open hatch in the floor.

Davy rushed to see. Uh oh! The cannonball had fallen right down into the hold and through the hull.

Water bubbled up through the hole it had made.

Just then, Davy heard the Captain coming. In a panic, he closed the hatch.

"Everything OK, Davy?"
the Captain asked.

"Err, yes, Cap'n," Davy replied.
"Nearly finished."

"Arr. Well done," the Captain replied.
"I do like a clean cannonball. There'll be
extra sausages for you tonight.
Come on, leave the rest. Let's go and eat."

But Davy couldn't eat. He was worried about the leak in the hold. Why hadn't he told the Captain? "Is everything OK, Davy?" kind Sam asked. "Did you know that Pete keeps stealing your sausages?"

"Everything's fine," Davy replied quickly. "I'm just tired. I think I'll have an early night."

But everything wasn't fine. Davy couldn't sleep. What if the ship sank? But he was too embarrassed to tell the captain. After all, the captain had told him to be careful. He felt so stupid.

At first light, he snuck carefully out of his hammock, taking care not to wake Pete, and went down to the hold.

He opened the hatch to find the hold
full of water! The *Golden Duck* rolled
slowly in the stormy sea. They were sinking.
"I've got to own up," he said to himself.

Bravely, he went
to see the captain.
  "I'm sorry, Captain," Davy began in a rush.
"But yesterday I dropped a cannonball and
it caused a leak, but I didn't tell you and now
the hold is full of water and I'm very, very sorry."

"Blistering barnacles.
This is terrible.
ALL HANDS ON DECK!"
the Captain cried out.

The other pirates came running,
rubbing their eyes.
  "What is it, Captain?" Pete asked.
The Captain told them what
had happened.

"I'm very, very, very sorry," Davy said.
"No time to feel sorry," shouted
the Captain. "We need to save the ship!"

"Nell, dive down and plug the leak,"
the Captain ordered. "Pete and Sam, start
baling the hold. Davy, you come with me."

Nell dived down and plugged the leak
with an old pair of bloomers.

Pete and Sam baled water with huge buckets.

Davy trimmed the sails while the Captain turned the wheel, sailing them into calmer waters. Working together as a team, the pirates saved the ship!

"I'm sorry I dropped the cannonball,"
Davy said afterwards.
"We all make mistakes," Nell said,
still dripping with seawater.
"I needed a bath anyway."

"I should have said 'I did it' straight away,"
Davy said, eyes down.
"Yes, you should have," the Captain agreed.
"But your bravery in owning up saved the ship."

"And, now that we've had all that water sloshing in the hold," the Captain continued, "we'll have the cleanest cannonballs on the seven seas!"

NOTES FOR PARENTS AND TEACHERS

Pirates to the Rescue

The books in the 'Pirates to the Rescue' series are designed to help children recognise the virtues of generosity, honesty, politeness and kindness.
Reading these books will show children that their actions and behaviour have a real effect on people around them, helping them to recognise what is right and wrong, and to think about what to do when faced with difficult choices.

I Did It!

'I Did It' is intended to be an engaging and enjoyable read for children aged 4-7. The book will help children recognise why it's important to be honest and that owning up is not only the right thing to do, but is the easiest choice in the long-term.

Teaching children to be honest will take time and is likely to be an ongoing lesson for many years. The natural inclination of many children is to deny responsibility and seek to escape blame. Very young children may even tell fibs for entertainment value. On the other hand, children sometimes tend to tell the complete, unblemished truth even when it's not required. It's important that children learn that being honest should be tempered by manners.

Admonishing children who make mistakes, hurt one another or damage family property is a reasonable and correct approach, but it does leave children feeling anxious about bringing such transgression to the attention of the parent. It is important for parents to reinforce the notion that honesty is a virtue in itself and that it can help to mitigate the damage caused. Make a point of thanking your child for their honesty. Explain that it doesn't make it right, but that owning up will certainly reduce the severity of the punishment, for example, 'Mummy's still angry, but she would have been even more angry if you hadn't owned up.'

Suggested follow-up activities

Ask your child to put him or herself in the position of Pete when he discovers the dropped cannonball has caused a leak. How does he feel when he wakes to find the ship is in real danger? What is the result of Davy's confession? Discuss how the crew react? Why do they think the Captain decides not punish Davy?

Take time to explain what honesty is, and what a lie is. Try to instil in your child a desire to do the right thing. Make a values chart writing on all the virtues you and your child can think of. Put a sticker on the chart every time your child is honest and displays one of the virtues listed.

Notice and praise acts of honesty from your child, however minor. Say 'I'm pleased you were honest and told me you spilled the drink. Now let's clean this up ogether.' Some children who learn the value of honesty can go through a phase of telling tales. Make a point of explaining about personal responsibility. It can be difficult for a child to judge when to tell a teacher about misbehaving peers and when to keep out of it! Explain to your child that taking responsibility sometimes means trying to sort matters out themselves.

Don't forget to be honest with your partner, or your child's older siblings. Make a show of it. Avoid lying to your child, even about difficult subjects like illness or death. If you break a glass, or leave the top off the toothpaste, own up! Young children watch and imitate adult behaviour. Tell your child what you are going to do and why, for example, 'Daddy broke Mummy's favourite vase. I'll tell her as soon as she gets in from work and buy her a new one.'

BOOKS TO SHARE

Come Clean, Carlos: Tell the Truth (You Choose)
by Sarah Eason (Wayland, 2013)

The 'You Choose' series explores dilemmas that all children face.
Amusing and simple multiple choice questions encourage children to look
at different ways to resolve situations and decide which choice they would
make, while helping the character in the book choose the RIGHT thing to do.

I Didn't Do It!: A Book About Telling the Truth (Our Emotions)
by Sue Graves (Watts, 2013)

Poppy doesn't always tell the truth at home. She doesn't always tell
the truth at school either. Now she's getting other children into trouble.
Can she learn that it's better to own up than to tell a lie?

It's Wasn't Me!
by Brian Moses (Wayland, 2008)

This amusing picture book, also illustrated by Mike Gordon, looks at
why we tell lies and how telling lies leads to trouble. It also considers
the grey area of telling a white lie, coping with angry feelings when
people tell lies about you, and having the courage to be honest.
This book is one of a series which help children to develop their
own value system and make responsible decisions.
Notes for parents and teachers show how ideas in the
books can be used as starting points for further
discussion, at home, in the classroom or in assemblies.

Read all the books in this series:

Aye Aye Captain!: Pirates Can Be Polite
978 0 7502 8296 3

Captain Cod is fed up. His crew are rude and not very polite to him at all. When the ship is attacked by a band of Rotten Pirates, the crew don't know what to do. They rush to the Captain's cabin to ask for advice, but his door is locked and he won't answer. Will the ship be overrun with Rotten Pirates? Or could good manners save the day?

Helping Polly Parrot!: Pirates Can Be Kind
978 0 7502 8297 0

Polly Parrot loves being a pirate parrot, but sometimes life on board ship is quite hard. All the other pirates have somewhere cosy to sleep, yet nobody cares that Polly hasn't got a place to rest. Will a near disaster help the pirate crew realise that they should be more kind and thoughtful?

I Did It!: Pirates Can Be Honest
978 0 7502 8295 6

Despite being told to be careful, poor pirate Davy starts daydreaming and drops a huge cannonball right through the ship's hull. Davy is too embarrassed to tell anyone and goes to bed. The next morning, the ship is filling with water and starting to sink. Will Davy be honest enough to own up and save the ship from sinking?

Treasure Ahoy!: Pirates Can Share
978 0 7502 8298 7

Lucky pirate Sam finds a bag of gold coins buried in the sand. He hides them in his pocket and keeps his fantastic find secret from everyone else. That night, he imagines what he might spend his booty on. But then he remembers all the things that the other pirates need. Will Sam decide it's good to share?